The SINGING TORTOISE

The SINGING TORTOISE

And Other Animal Folktales

by JOHN YEOMAN
pictures by QUENTIN BLAKE

TAMBOURINE BOOKS · NEW YORK

Text copyright ©1993 by John Yeoman
Illustrations copyright © 1993 by Quentin Blake
First published in Great Britain by Victor Gollancz, an imprint of Cassell
Printed in Singapore

Library of Congress Cataloging in Publication Data
Yeoman, John. The singing tortoise and other animal folktales/by John Yeoman;
illustrated by Quentin Blake. —1st U.S. ed. p. cm. Contents: The crocodile and the jackal—
The young leopard and the ram—The coyote and the ravens—The singing tortoise—The
impudent little bird—The turkey girl—How the turtle got his shell—The Ranee and the
cobra—The cat and the mice—Animal language—The rabbit and the elephants.
1. Animals—Folklore. 2. Tales. [1. Animals—Folklore. 2. Folklore.] I. Blake, Quentin,
ill. II. Title. PZ8.1.Y35Si 1994 398.24'5—dc20 93-31208 CIP AC
ISBN 0-688-13366-5 (trade)
First U.S. edition, 1994
1 3 5 7 9 10 8 6 4 2

Contents

The Crocodile and the Jackal

ONE DAY the jackal discovered a new stretch of the riverbank where there were plenty of mud crabs for him to eat. What he hadn't discovered was that this was the favorite spot of a very large crocodile. But the crocodile had discovered him, and was looking forward to eating him.

The jackal was so intent on catching a crab that was scurrying toward the shelter of the bulrushes that he didn't see the crocodile lurking there.

The first he knew was the sound of the crocodile's snapping jaws and the feeling that his paw was trapped.

"I must think of something quickly," he told himself. "Otherwise, he will pull me under the water, and first drown me and then eat me."

An idea occurred to him. "You must have very poor eyesight, crocodile," he said in as cheerful a voice as he could manage. "You seem to have caught hold of a mouthful of bulrush root, when I imagine you were hoping to take a bite out of me."

"Drat!" snarled the crocodile to himself, releasing his hold.

At once the jackal sprang higher up the bank to safety. "Fooled you there, crocodile," he mocked. "You'll have to try harder next time."

The crocodile knew that the jackal was too far out of reach now, but vowed to himself that he certainly would try harder next time.

The next day the jackal was more cautious when he returned to the riverbank. For all his brave words on the previous day, he'd had a nasty shock.

"Where shall I start?" he said, as if thinking aloud. "I wonder if I can see where the juicy little crabs are, by their bubbles? They always make bubbles when they are resting in the mud."

Now the crocodile heard this, just as he was meant to, and decided to entice the jackal toward him by imitating a crab. Bringing his snout to just below the surface of the water, he began to blow with all his might.

He produced a great rush of bubbles that swirled in a whirlpool.

"Thank you for letting me know where you are, crocodile!" called the jackal. "I think I'll eat my meal further along the bank, after all," he said, running off.

The crocodile was furious, and even more determined to catch the jackal. But he realized that the jackal would always be on the alert when he came down to the water.

"I know, I'll catch him on land," he said. "I'll grab him when he goes gathering figs. He'll never expect to see me there."

So early the next morning the crocodile made his way to the wild fig grove, where masses of ripe figs had fallen. Not knowing where best to hide, he pushed a lot of the figs into a heap with his snout and burrowed inside it, covering his body as best he could.

When the jackal came along he stopped in surprise. There, ahead of him, was a very tempting pile of freshly fallen figs, but they were in a heap that looked suspiciously like the shape of a crocodile.

"What a lot of figs this morning," he said aloud. "And yet I don't think they can be the juicy little ones that I like to eat. The ones I prefer are so delicate that they roll here and there in the breeze."

"If that's all he wants," thought the crocodile, "I can easily oblige." And he waggled his bottom vigorously, sending the figs flying in every direction.

"Oh, I didn't mean to disturb you at your meal, crocodile," the jackal called over his shoulder, as he scampered off.

The crocodile knew that it was hopeless to give chase on dry land. But he was more determined than ever to catch this impudent creature who kept making fun of him.

"I'll wait for him at his den," he said. "He's bound to go back there this evening."

When the jackal reached home, after an undisturbed meal of crabs, he soon noticed that he had had a visitor. There were deep claw marks in the grass and there were signs that some large animal had been trying to squeeze itself through the narrow entrance to the den.

The jackal was taking no chances. "What have I done to offend you, little house?" he called. "This is the first time you've not greeted me on my return."

In what he hoped was a sweet little voice, the crocodile rasped, "Welcome home, master. Do come in."

"Aha," said the jackal to himself. "I begin to regret teasing the crocodile so much. He is becoming very persistent and may well catch me one of these days, if I don't frighten him off once and for all."

"I'll be with you presently, little house," he called. "I must just collect some firewood so that I can prepare my evening meal."

In no time at all the jackal had gathered up a great pile of sticks, which he then set alight and pushed into the den with the help of a fallen branch.

Within seconds the crocodile was pushing his way out through the smoke, coughing and gasping and rubbing his eyes. The jackal smiled to himself as he heard him crashing through the bushes on his way down to the river.

And the crocodile never troubled the jackal again.

The Young Leopard and the Ram

A YOUNG LEOPARD was on his way home after an unsuccessful day's hunting when he found himself face to face with a huge ram. Now the leopard had never seen such a creature before and had no idea whether it was ferocious or not.

Thinking it best to play safe he said, "Good afternoon, friend. I don't think we've met before. May I ask your name?"

The ram, of course, knew very well what leopards were like and decided that the best way to protect himself was to put on a brave face.

"I am the great ram," he bleated, in his loudest voice, "the terror of the bush. And who are you, might I ask, and what business do you have in this territory?"

"Oh, I am only a leopard, sir," said the young animal, quaking all over. "And I was just passing through. If it's all the same to you, I'll be going now."

And with that the leopard bounded off as fast as his trembling legs would carry him.

A mile or so away the jackal stumbled upon the leopard as he lay, nervous and panting, in the undergrowth.

"What on earth's the matter?" asked the jackal, thinking there might be some danger about.

"Oh, my friend," gasped the leopard, "I can't tell you what a narrow escape I've just had. Imagine it: I came face to face with the great ram, the terror of the bush."

"You young fool," said the jackal. "You've just missed the chance of a first-rate meal." Then he thought for a moment.

"You know," he said, "if only you could take me to the spot where you bumped into him we might both get a meal out of it. I'll see you tomorrow."

In admiration the leopard watched the jackal trot away, and only wished that he were as brave as that.

Since the jackal knew that the leopard would try to talk himself out of going back to see the ram, he decided he would have to bully him into it.

"Look," he said, when he returned the following day. "I've brought a leather strap. If I tie one end round your neck and the other round my waist, like this, we'll be able to keep together, and you won't have any reason to feel nervous."

The leopard didn't look convinced but allowed the jackal to lead him back along the track, all the same.

As they approached, the ram lifted his head and sniffed the air.

"My dear," he said quietly to his wife, "I'm afraid that these may be our last minutes. I can smell the leopard in the air and I don't think he'll be so easily fooled a second time."

His wife, though, had an idea. "There is just one chance," she said, "if you take the child." And she nuzzled their lamb toward its father and whispered something in the ram's ear.

At that moment the jackal and the leopard burst through the undergrowth. A violent twitching on the leather strap told the jackal that his young companion was having second thoughts.

But the jackal knew that the strap was fastened tightly and that the leopard couldn't creep away, no matter how badly he wanted to.

What the jackal didn't know was how brave the ram would turn out to be in this moment of danger.

"Oh, thank you, jackal," said the ram, in a remarkably steady voice. "My wife and I were at our wits' end to know how to feed the baby, for it simply turns its nose up at the grass we offer it and refuses to eat anything but leopard."

Unseen by the others, the ewe then gave the baby's bottom a gentle nip, at which it let out an ear-splitting bleat.

This was altogether too much for the young leopard. He screamed, turned on his heels and dashed headlong into the bushes, dragging the unfortunate jackal after him.

The leopard had been so terrified by the encounter and the jackal had been so bumped and bruised by his homeward journey that the two of them left the ram and his family well alone after that.

The Coyote and the Ravens

A LONG, LONG TIME AGO, in the Canyon of the Cedars, there lived a coyote.

One day he went out, telling his family that he was going hunting, although his wife and children knew perfectly well that he was only going out for a stroll to see what was going on.

He ambled over toward Thunder Mountain, dragging his tail behind him carelessly, and began to scramble up the loose rocks of the foothills.

Now it just happened that this trail led past a little column of rock with a rounded top, and perched on this rock were two old ravens having an eye-race.

They did it like this. With his beak one of them would point out a pinnacle on the slope on the opposite side of the valley. Then he would croak:

Swift and sure as the raven flies,
Round that rock will go my eyes.

At this, by lowering his head, craning forward, and squeezing with all his might–*pop*–he would force his eyes out of their sockets and send them whizzing across the valley, making a turn round the rock, and then speeding back to him.

As they approached, the raven would swell up his throat and make a long *whooooh* noise, ready to receive his eyes back in their sockets with a soft *thunk!*

And then the other raven would choose another column of rock to aim at and do exactly the same, after which they would laugh themselves silly and ruffle their feathers up.

From a distance the coyote heard one of the ravens making his *whooooh* noise, as he hummed his eyes back to him, and then the loud peals of raucous laughter that followed, and this put him in a good mood. Sticking his tail up straight, he trotted forward briskly until he arrived at the foot of their column.

"Good morning, friends," he said in the grating, high-pitched voice that coyotes use when they want to make themselves agreeable. "I'm glad to see that you're enjoying yourselves."

At this the ravens burst out laughing again and punched one another in a good-natured way.

"Would you be so kind as to tell me what it is that you find so entertaining?" asked the coyote, half-hoping to be invited to join in.

"We're having eye-races," said one of the ravens.

"Eye-races? How on earth do you have an eye-race?" asked the coyote, bewildered.

"Do you mean you don't know what an eye-race is?" asked the other raven. Then, turning to his companion, he said, "I really do believe he's never done any eye-racing in his life."

"Then we shall have to show him," said the first raven, getting into his starting position. "You see that tall standing rock right across the valley? Well,

> Swift and sure as the raven flies,
> Round that rock will go my eyes."

And once again, by lowering his head, craning forward, and squeezing with all his might, he popped his eyes out.

The coyote watched dumbfounded as they sped across the valley and round the rock, and then came speeding back toward them.

Whooooh, went the raven, and then came the *thunk!* as his eyes slipped back in again.

"By the moon," exclaimed the coyote, "that is one of the most extraordinary and comical things I've ever seen in my life. No wonder you were laughing so much. Teach me how to do that. I've got to know how to do that."

And without waiting for an invitation, he puffed and panted his way up to the top of the column, pushing the ravens aside to make room for himself to squat down.

"Now, what do I have to do?" he asked.

"Well," said the first raven, "you just stick your head forward like this, and–"

"All right, all right, I know. I saw you, didn't I?" said the coyote.

Now that is absolutely typical of a coyote. Always asking people for favors and never showing the least bit of gratitude.

Well, he hunched himself up, and squeezed and strained and groaned, and got absolutely nowhere. So he had to ask the ravens to explain again.

"You have to strain with all your neck muscles and stretch your eyelids apart as far as you can, and–"

"Well, what do you think I'm doing?" the coyote snapped, rudely interrupting the first raven.

"I think it would be easier the first time," said the other raven, giving his friend a wink, "if you allow us to help you. Just get back into the straining position, please."

The coyote did this and, quick as a flash, the ravens each tweaked out one of his eyes and sent it whizzing across the valley like a pea from a peashooter.

"There, you've done it," they said. "With a little help."

And at this they flew off in pursuit of the coyote's eyes, caught up with them, and swallowed them, laughing fit to burst all the time.

The coyote, who had no idea of the trick the ravens had played on him, sat waiting for what he imagined was the right length of time, and then started making a *whooooh* noise, expecting to feel his eyes plop back into place.

He *whooooohed* and *whooooohed* until his throat was sore, and finally realized that his eyes weren't going to come back.

"Oh, no," he whined. "They've got lost, and I'll have to try and find them if I ever want to hunt again."

With his front paws he gingerly felt around him (for remember, he was perched on a narrow column of rock) and slithered and slid as best he could, landing in a heap in the dust.

Feeling his way step by step he finally reached a damp area through which one of the valley springs runs. Here he blundered into a bush and knocked off one of its yellow, ripening berries. He heard it strike the ground.

"What's that?" he cried excitedly, feeling around for it with his paw. "Ah, here it is!" he said. "It's one of my eyes!" And he slipped it into one of his empty sockets.

It wasn't long before he discovered another fallen berry, and popped that into place, too.

He was slightly disappointed that he couldn't see as well as before– everything seemed rather blurry–but he put that down to the fact that his eyes must have got very dusty on their journey.

The most important thing for him was that he had got his eyes back again. And he was off home with a great feeling of relief.

As I told you, this happened a long, long time ago, but to this day all coyotes have yellow eyes and have some difficulty seeing.

That's the long and short of it.

The Singing Tortoise

O NE DAY, a hunter who had been following a trail which had gone cold, found himself in an unfamiliar part of the forest. Stopping to get his bearings by the sun, he was suddenly aware of a gentle voice, sweetly singing:

Man fights to keep alive, or so they say;
Night and day, night and day.
And yet the truth is quite the other way:
Man is the hunter; all the world's his prey.
Night and day.

The song was accompanied by very delicate music which completely captivated the hunter. Curious to find the singer, he carefully pushed aside the branches and found, to his amazement, a tortoise with a tiny harp slung round her neck. She didn't seem in the least put out by her audience and continued her song.

The hunter was so taken with his discovery that he returned to the same isolated spot day after day to listen to the remarkable creature.

Finally, he simply had to ask her if he could convey her back to his hut so that he could enjoy her singing in comfort, at any time of day.

At first she looked doubtful but then, seeing his disappointed face, she agreed.

"But," she said, "this is on condition that I sing for you, and you alone."

The hunter agreed willingly and carried his precious discovery back to his hut, where he saw to it that she had the tenderest leaves to eat and the freshest water to drink.

But although he had meant to keep the promise which he had made to the tortoise, he began desperately to wish that he could let the rest of the world know his wonderful secret. To tell the truth, he thought it would bring him great honor in the community.

After a few weeks the temptation became too strong for him and he confided the secret to first one friend and then another, until–of course–the story reached the ears of the chief himself.

Immediately a great assembly was called, and the hunter was summoned to appear before it.

Slightly anxious, but also very satisfied with himself, he described the tortoise and the way she sang and played.

The crowd laughed and jeered in disbelief, until the chief silenced them.

"This is hard to believe without proof," he said.

Without thinking, the hunter replied, "If I am not speaking the truth, I will give you leave to kill me. Tomorrow I shall bring the tortoise to the assembly place, that everyone may see and hear her. If you disbelieve me then, I am quite prepared to die."

"That is good," said a voice from the crowd. It was the man who had led the mockery. "And if she can do as you say, you have our leave to punish us in any way you think fit. That is only just."

The matter being settled, the chief dismissed the assembly and the hunter returned home well-satisfied with the outcome.

At dawn the following day he appeared with the tortoise and her harp at the assembly place where an enormous crowd had already gathered.

He gently placed the tortoise on a cane table which had been provided for her, and a complete hush fell over the gathering.

There was silence. The people were straining forward attentively to hear, but there was nothing to hear.

Everyone was prepared to be patient; they were quite willing to give the tortoise a chance, knowing that she might be nervous, but hours went by and there was still silence.

The hunter gave the tortoise pleading looks but, to his dismay and shame, she stayed motionless and mute.

Gradually, faint whispers began to run through the crowd; and then they turned into discontented muttering, which finally gave way to an outburst of anger and scorn.

The hunter's fate was sealed with the setting of the sun. There in the assembly place, as the last ray faded, he was beheaded.

Through the silence that followed the execution came a little voice, which said:

"And yet he told you the truth."

The crowd turned to stare at the tortoise in amazement and shock.

"We have killed him, and he was telling the truth," repeated the chief, rising to his feet in horror.

The tortoise went on, "And yet he brought his punishment upon himself. I led a happy life in the forest, singing and playing all day. And he knew that I was quite content for him to come and listen to me. But that did not satisfy him. He had to tell the secret (which was not his to tell) to the world. If he had not tried to win your admiration by making a show of me this would never have happened." And, in an indescribably sad voice, she sang:

> *Man fights to keep alive, or so they say;*
> *Night and day, night and day.*
> *And yet the truth is quite the other way:*
> *Man is the hunter; all the world's his prey.*
> *Night and day.*

From that day on she thought it better not to sing.

The Impudent Little Bird

THERE WAS ONCE an impudent little bird who went to a tailor and ordered a little woollen coat. He chose the cloth and picked an attractive design. Then he held his wings up while the tailor took his measurements.

After that he went to the hatter and ordered himself a handsome little hat, and then to the shoemaker and ordered a fashionable pair of shoes.

And the bird was so conceited that when the coat and the hat and the shoes were ready for him to pick up he just said, "Send me the bill," and flew off without paying. This left the tailor, the hatter, and the shoemaker feeling very annoyed.

The little bird considered himself so fetching in his new things that he thought he'd go and show himself off in the palace gardens. He perched on a branch by the open window of the banqueting room, where the King was dining, and sang at the top of his voice:

> *No wonder I whistle; no wonder I sing–*
> *I'm dressed*
> *In my best,*
> *And I look like a king.*

At first the King was rather amused to hear this, but after the fifth time it began to irritate him a little, and at the five-hundredth time it made him very annoyed indeed.

"Someone silence that impudent little bird!" he thundered. "I order him to be caught and plucked and cooked and served to me at once."

When the King gave orders, especially when he gave orders in an angry voice, he was immediately obeyed.

Without its feathers the bird looked so tiny on the King's plate that he said, "I shall swallow you whole, just to teach you a lesson for your impertinence." And he did.

The little bird was highly indignant at having been treated like this, and not being able to see his way down there in the dark, he began to kick in all directions to be let out.

Now although the bird had only tiny legs, he had very pointed little claws and so his kicking made the King feel distinctly uncomfortable.

In no time the royal stomachache doctor arrived with a bottle of red medicine.

"Open your mouth, Your Majesty, and hold your nose. It doesn't taste very nice, but that's how you know it's doing you good."

In fact, the medicine tasted so unpleasant that the little bird waited for the King's mouth to open for a second time and then, to everyone's amazement, flew straight out at breakneck speed.

He headed straight for a fountain, where he washed himself clean, and then perched on a branch to dry himself off and examine the damage.

His little heart sank when he looked down at his featherless body. To think that only that morning he had been the best-dressed bird in the kingdom.

Although the other birds all thought he was a show-off, they still felt sorry for him, and when he begged for a few feathers to cover himself with, everyone willingly gave him one.

He darted over to the royal carpenter's shop and rolled around in the glue for a bit before beginning to stick feathers onto himself.

It didn't matter to him that the feathers were all of different sizes and different colors. In fact, when he looked at his reflection in the pool of the fountain, he was convinced that he was even more elegant than he had been in his new clothes that morning.

He was so pleased with himself that he couldn't resist flying back to the tree outside the banqueting room, where the King was just peeling himself an orange to take the nasty taste away.

Looking like an exploded rainbow, the little bird burst into song at the top of his voice:

> *The King tried to eat me; I made him feel sick.*
> *He popped me in fast, but I popped out as quick!*

The King rose, overturning his chair.

"That impudent little bird," he stormed. "Catch him again, pluck him again, chop him into pieces, and cook him again!"

But the little bird was having none of that. Instead, he flew like the wind and didn't stop until he landed on the nose of the man in the moon.

The Turkey Girl

IN THE DIM DISTANT PAST the people of Matsaki, the Salt City, didn't keep sheep or horses or cattle, but they did keep turkeys. In fact, some of the wealthy families owned such large flocks that they employed poor people to look after them on the surrounding plains.

At the very edge of the town in a tumbledown, one-room shack there lived all alone a very poor girl who earned her living, such as it was, in this way. Although she had bright eyes and a sweet smile her clothes were tattered and dirty, for she was given no money for her work–just scraps of food and the odd cast-off garment.

Having no companions to talk to she relieved her loneliness by lavishing her kindness on the turkeys in her care. And in return, seeing what a good helper they had, the turkeys grew so fond of her that they would obey her every command. They never fought among themselves, they never strayed, and they always returned obediently to their cage when the sun was ready to set.

One day, as the turkey girl was driving her flock across the plain, she saw a herald priest on a housetop and listened to what he had to proclaim.

His message traveled loud and clear across the plains–in four days' time the ceremonial Bird Dance was to be held in Zuñi.

At first the turkey girl was full of excitement because this was a festival where all the youths and maidens were allowed to join in. But then she remembered how everyone would be dressed in their

41

beautiful ceremonial costumes and realized that they would be unwilling to let her even watch, let alone join in, the dance.

Out of habit she said all this to her turkeys as they went along, and told them how disappointed she was.

In the days leading up to the festival the countryside was alive with activities. At each little house the poor turkey girl saw people cleaning and mending their splendid garments, or preparing delicacies for the feast, or making decorations for the streets. Everyone was so busy and so happy that it made her feel even more alone and unwanted, as she told her birds.

On the day of the festival as she drove her flock down to the plain, Matsaki was almost deserted because the people had all left early in order to reach Zuñi in good time.

The turkey girl was wandering along deep in thought, trying to imagine the crowds swarming happily through the town and the music and the laughter, when her daydream was suddenly interrupted.

The largest turkey strutted up to her and, fanning out his tail and spreading out his wings like a skirt, said (in his bubbly voice):

"Maiden mother, we know how you feel and we truly pity you. At night, in our cage, we have been talking about you. We feel that it is unfair that all the people of Matsaki should go to the celebrations in Zuñi and leave you behind, so we have decided on a plan to help you.

"Early this afternoon when the Bird Dance is just beginning, you must drive us all back to our cage. There we shall make you the most beautifully dressed young woman in the land. And you shall go to Zuñi, and everyone will admire you, and–most of all–the young men will beg you to join hands with them in the circle of the dance."

At first the turkey girl could not believe that a turkey could be talking to her in this way, but after a while it seemed the most natural thing in the world.

"But are you sure that you can do this, my dear turkeys?" she asked. "I don't think I could bear it if my hopes were raised for nothing."

"Trust us," said the big turkey. And all the others nodded. "But I must tell you one important thing," he continued. "There is no knowing how much future happiness and good fortune will come of this if you can enjoy today's pleasures with moderation. But if you allow yourself to get carried away and forget about us, your true friends, in your excitement, then we have no choice but to leave you to your hard life. We should be forced to think, 'If our maiden mother were more prosperous, she would only treat others as others treat her now.' And that would be a great shame."

"Have no fear, my dear turkeys," she cried. "Out of love and gratitude I shall do exactly as you tell me, and you shall be in my thoughts every moment of the dance."

Well before the sun had begun to sink the turkeys set off homeward with one accord, followed by the turkey girl. Her head was so light she seemed to be walking in a dream.

At the edge of the town the large turkey made a low bow and humbly begged her to enter their cage. She ducked her head and entered the long wooden shed in which all the other turkeys had taken up their places.

"First you must give me your mantle," said the large turkey.

Blushing for shame because it was so torn and so dirty she slipped it off and placed it on the floor in front of him.

She watched in wonder while he strutted and stamped upon it, finally lowering himself to fan it with his outspread wing feathers. At last he rose and, picking up the mantle in his beak, presented it to her.

Instead of the tattered article she had given him, she found herself holding a sweet-smelling mantle of beautiful white embroidered cotton. As she placed it over her shoulders her appearance was completely transformed.

With the turkeys strutting about her in a circle and clucking in celebration, she discovered that all her clothes had become pretty and fresh, that her skin had become soft and clean, and her hair had become fine and silky.

All the turkeys clucked their praise and their best wishes and she left the cage to start on her journey.

"One more thing, little maiden mother," said the large turkey. "Do not fasten the door of the cage. For who can know whether you will spare a thought for your turkeys or whether, indeed, you may not grow ashamed to remember that you have been our keeper. We love you and dearly wish you good fortune but remember, you may not stay too long."

"How could I forget!" said the turkey girl, blowing them all a kiss before setting off.

She ran as fast as her feet would take her toward Zuñi and heard the sounds of music and laughter well before she reached the town.

Just pausing to recover her breath she slipped in through one of the covered ways that led into the dance court. As she passed along, all heads turned and she heard murmurs of astonishment at her beauty and at the richness of her attire. But nobody recognized her.

The chiefs of the dance, splendid in their ceremonial garments, quickly invited her to join the youths and maidens dancing round the musicians in the center of the court.

Smiling and blushing and tossing back her hair, she took her place in the circle, where the young men jostled to dance beside her. Her heart fluttered and her face glowed as the music swept her off her feet, and it seemed to her that no time at all had passed when the sun sank below the rooftops.

She was so filled with excitement that if she thought of her turkeys it was only to say to herself, "I can surely spend another hour or two of enjoyment before I need to return. They surely wouldn't want me to miss the fun of hearing everyone wondering who the girl was, who turned every head at the Bird Dance."

And so time passed, and another dance was announced, and another; and the young men wouldn't let her rest, but begged her to join in every one.

At last, when the fires were burning low and the visitors from Matsaki were beginning to drift off home, she knew she must now break away. Being swift of foot and knowing the little-used tracks, she was able to disappear into the darkness and reach the outskirts of town without being seen.

But by now the turkeys had become anxious. Finally, the large turkey dropped down from his perch and addressed them all:

"We were wrong to expect so much. She has forgotten us and has shown that she is not worthy of anything better than that she has been used to. Our task is done, and we may as well take to the mountains and free ourselves from this dreary captivity."

So, clucking to one another in the darkness, they filed out of their cage and trooped off toward the Cottonwoods Canyon, round behind Thunder Mountain, and then on up the valley.

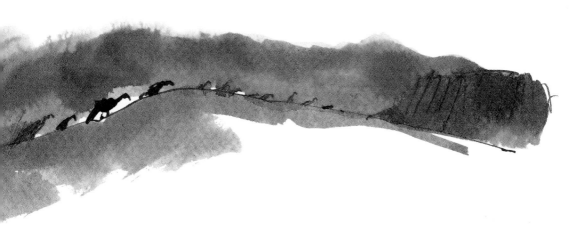

When the turkey girl arrived, exhausted but eager to tell her turkeys of the wonders of the dance, she found the cage empty. Catching the faint sound of their voices in the blackness she stumbled along behind them. From time to time she could make out snatches of their song:

> *K'yaanaa to! to!*
> *K'yaanaa to! to!*
> *Yee huli! huli!*

Hearing this, the turkey girl called out, pleading with them to stop; but she called in vain. Through the night air came the sound of their flapping wings as they lifted and took flight toward the Zuñi Mountains.

The poor turkey girl turned and stumbled slowly back home. And in the growing light she saw what she had half-feared to see–she was once again wearing her old tattered clothes.

Since that time turkeys have always been found in large numbers along the plains that border the Zuñi Mountains. And the local people still have a saying that goes: "Life sends you what you deserve. If you are poor in feeling as well as in money, then you must expect to stay poor."

That, sadly, is the long and short of it.

How the Turtle Got His Shell

THIS IS A STORY from the days when the animals were all what the Papuans call *bariawa*, and spoke and behaved just as humans do now.

A long time ago, longer ago than any of us can remember, the turtle and the wallaby were friends. In those days the turtle had no shell and so he could move more quickly, and had no trouble trotting along behind his companion.

One afternoon, when they were sunning themselves on the beach, the turtle suddenly announced that he felt very hungry.

The wallaby thought a bit and then said, "I have an idea. Let's creep into Binama's garden and eat some of his sugarcane and bananas. He'll never know."

The turtle was uncertain at first. Binama the hornbill had a ferocious temper and was proud of his garden–but the thought of sugarcane and bananas was very tempting.

"All right, then," he said. "But we must be careful not to be seen."

They tiptoed across the sand to the gate and peered through the bars. There was no one about, so they let themselves in.

To make things easier for his friend, the wallaby trampled down the stems of the sugarcane and bent the stalks of the bananas. They had never had such a feast.

Now, about this time all the birds were returning from their gardens with the taro roots which they had dug up for their evening meal.

51

They gathered in the village compound and set about peeling the roots and cutting them up for the pot.

Suddenly Binama the hornbill said, "Someone must go down to the beach to fetch some seawater for us to cook with. We want our taro to be nice and salty."

The birds secretly agreed, but no one offered to go. They were frightened that there might be some enemy lying in wait on the way.

One by one they invented excuses until finally the brave little wagtail put them all to shame by saying, "Well, if no one else is prepared to fetch the water, I suppose I shall have to go."

But he was taking no chances. Before he set out with his bottles he hung his shell breastplate round his neck, tied a bunch of waving feathers round his head, and took up his spear.

And to make himself feel even safer he skipped from side to side as he made his way toward the beach—to confuse any enemy that might be lurking in the undergrowth.

When they caught sight of him bobbing along beside the hornbill's garden the wallaby and the turtle were overcome with fear. But the turtle managed to say, "Please don't be surprised to find us in your master's garden. Binama was kind enough to invite us to help ourselves."

The wagtail was clever enough to pretend that he believed the turtle, and simply bowed before continuing on his way to the water's edge. But he knew that the turtle had not been telling the truth.

As soon as he had filled his bottles with seawater he skipped back to the village by another path, and told the other birds what he had seen.

"How dare the wallaby and the turtle steal food from our master," they cried. "We'll soon put a stop to that!" And taking their spears they flocked down to Binama's garden and surrounded it.

When he saw what was happening the wallaby gave a tremendous leap which sent him soaring above their heads, and he bounded away into the bushes.

The unfortunate turtle could do nothing but scamper into the shelter of a yam patch, where the trembling leaves soon gave him away.

As the birds dragged him out he pleaded with them for mercy. "It wasn't my fault," he whimpered. "It was the wallaby who broke all the stalks down and . . ." But the birds weren't interested in his excuses and hauled him off to Binama's house. The hornbill ordered him to be tied up and put on a shelf until the following day.

The next morning Binama announced that there was to be a great feast at which they would slay the turtle, and he ordered all the birds to make preparations.

When the horrified turtle noticed that everyone had gone out to the gardens to collect food and that only the young hornbills were left in the house to guard him he decided on a plan.

"Sweet little masters," he said in a gentle voice, "if only you would be good enough to untie me, we could play a little game."

The young hornbills, not suspecting what was in his mind, undid the knots.

The turtle crawled down from the ledge, stretched his arms and legs a bit to relieve the cramps, and then said, "Shall we dress up? If you brought me all your best ornaments I could put them on."

The young hornbills eagerly showed him a basket full of Binama's most precious ornaments—a fine necklace of shell money, two shell armlets, and a carved wooden bowl.

They helped the turtle to wind the necklace round his neck and slip the armlets onto his arms and fasten the bowl on his back.

"I must look a wonderful sight," said the turtle. "I'll trot around for a while to show you how your father looks when he's dressed in his finery."

The young hornbills watched him waddle a few paces before calling him back. He returned at once to the shade of the tree under which the young birds were sitting.

"Well?" he asked. "How do I look?"

In fact he looked so ridiculous that the little hornbills could hardly
answer for laughing. They encouraged him to do it again, and he was
more than pleased to oblige.

When the young birds heard the others returning they called out
to the turtle to come back.

But it was too late. He had heard the others as well, and was making
a dash for the shore.

The children at last realized what was happening and shouted,
"Quick, quick; the turtle is escaping!"

The birds flung their bundles of food to the ground and set off after
the turtle, but he had already reached the sea and plunged in.

Binama and the angry birds knew that he must come up for air.
"Show yourself, turtle," they cried. "Lift up your head."

When the turtle came up for a breath, they hurled great stones at
him, and one shattered his left armlet before he dived for safety.

"Show yourself, turtle," they cried again. "Lift up your head."

When he came up for another breath, they hurled more stones and shattered his right armlet before he dived.

The third time they snapped the string of the necklace of shell money.

For the last time they cried, "Show yourself, turtle. Lift up your head." But no matter how many stones they rained down upon his back, they couldn't even make a dent in the solid wooden bowl.

In no time the turtle was out of sight, and an angry Binama led his followers back to the village.

And since then the turtle has always carried the hornbill's wooden bowl on his back.

The Ranee and the Cobra

O NCE UPON A TIME, in southern India, there lived a Rajah and a Ranee and their pet dog. The Rajah and the Ranee were very unhappy because they had no children, and their dog was very unhappy because she had no puppies.

One day, a palace servant ran to the Rajah to tell him that his dearest wish had been granted. But when the Rajah went to his wife's room he found that she had two little puppies. And to make matters worse, on the same day their pet dog had given birth to two beautiful little girls.

This made the Ranee very resentful and during the next few months she would often take her puppies down to the kennel, when the dog was in the kitchen having her dinner, and exchange them for the little girls. But it was no use; the dog always used to take her children back and return the puppies to their nursery.

The dog began to get very worried about the Ranee's jealousy, and one day she said to herself, "If the Ranee goes on upsetting my little girls like this it will make them ill. Much as I love them and much as I want them to live in comfort, I think I shall have to hide them in the jungle, for their own safety."

So that night she folded a cloth around the two children and, lifting it carefully in her mouth, slipped away with her precious bundle into the jungle. She found a clean, dry cave beside which ran a stream of crystal-clear water, and she settled them there.

Every day she would go into the town to steal food for her daughters. And whenever she could she would take pieces of beautiful cloth or delicate bracelets from the market stalls, for she was determined that even if her children were forced to live in the jungle they deserved nothing but the best.

Time passed and one day, when the mother dog was away getting food in the town, a young Rajah and his younger brother came hunting in that part of the jungle. Their hunt was exhausting and unsuccessful, and the day was extremely hot.

The young Rajah told his hunting party to rest in the shade and ordered his attendants to search for fresh water. They were away a long time and the courtiers were becoming very thirsty.

Suddenly the young Rajah noticed that one of his hunting dogs had a wet muzzle and wet paws. "He has found water," he said. "Someone follow him."

Two courtiers followed the hunting dog to the stream and, from a distance, saw the two beautifully dressed little girls. But the children also saw them and ran into their cave to hide, as their mother had taught them to do.

When the Princes heard of this they commanded the courtiers to lead them to the place, and were charmed by what they saw.

They were so charmed that at once each of them offered one of the little girls the protection of his palace, and begged the honor of the girl's hand in marriage when she should be old enough. The children were confused and frightened, but how could they refuse?

When the mother dog returned to the empty cave she grieved for the loss of her children, and for twelve long years the poor creature traveled the country looking for them.

One day, by chance, she arrived in the district where the two Princes had their palaces. As the dog padded down the street the daughter who was now a Ranee, the wife of the young Rajah, came to her window and saw her.

At first she could not believe her eyes, and then—when she was convinced that it really was her dear long-lost mother—she rushed down into the street and swept up the exhausted creature in her arms.

Back in her own room she wept over her, and hugged her and bathed her paws and settled her on a mound of silk cushions.

At last, when the old creature had recovered a little, she spoke:

"My dear daughter, words cannot express what your loving kindness means to me. But although it pains me to be separated from you for even a few hours, I feel that I must pay a visit to your sister now that my strength has returned. But never fear, I shall come back."

The Ranee, who knew her sister better than her mother did, wanted to dissuade her from going—but, feeling that this would be unkind, said nothing.

It just so happened the second daughter, now the wife of the younger Prince, was at her window when the dog appeared in the street below.

"Heavens," said the daughter to herself, "this old bedraggled creature is my mother. What shame and humiliation it would bring down on my head if my husband were ever to find out! I must do something, and quickly."

Immediately she ordered the servants to chase away the foul creature that was lurking outside.

"Throw stones at it," she commanded, "and throw them hard."

The servants did as they had been commanded and the old mother dog, bruised and bleeding from a cut on the head, only just managed to crawl back to her daughter, the Ranee, before collapsing.

The Ranee bathed her wounds and cradled her in her arms, and lamented that she had ever let her go to see her sister. But regrets were too late; the poor dog died.

Not only was the Ranee distressed at her mother's death; she was also fearful of what her husband, the Rajah, would say if he found a dead dog–an unclean animal–in his palace.

So she gently laid the body under an upturned basket in a small room which was rarely used, intending to give it a fitting and simple burial when she was alone the following day.

Unfortunately, the Rajah happened to pass through the room that evening and, seeing the basket, lifted it out of curiosity.

He called for a light to see what it was he had found and, lo and behold! There in front of him was a lifelike statue of a dog, composed entirely of gold and precious stones which blazed and sparkled in the flickering light.

He was amazed and asked his wife where she got such a beautiful and valuable object.

What could she say? She was so confused and frightened that, instead of telling her husband the whole truth, she simply said, "It came from my mother."

Now, as you know, the little fibs we tell to get ourselves out of difficulties often get us into even greater difficulties.

"But why didn't you speak of this before?" asked the Rajah in wonderment. "Why, this statue is worth the whole of my kingdom. Your parents must be very important people and it is only right that we should pay our respects to them immediately. Tell me, my love, where do they live?"

Now, as you know, when we tell one little fib we often find ourselves having to tell another.

"In the jungle," she said.

In no time the Rajah had ordered his courtiers to make preparations for a journey into the jungle to visit the Ranee's parents.

The Ranee dreaded to think what her husband would say when he found out that she had been telling such stories. She felt that he would have every right to cut off her head.

"You must allow me to set off in the palanquin first," she said. "They will wish to greet you with all honor and courtesy, and it is only right that I should tell them of your coming."

Little did the Rajah know that his poor wife was intending to go alone into the jungle to kill herself and put an end to her shame.

The attendants escorted the palanquin deep into the jungle. Peering through the curtains the Ranee saw a huge white ants' nest some way ahead, and next to it an open-mouthed cobra. A thought occurred to her, and she ordered the bearers to lower the palanquin and withdraw.

"I shall go up to the cobra," she decided, "and put my finger in its mouth so that it will bite me and I shall die."

Half-closing her eyes and summoning up all her courage, she approached the fearsome cobra.

She wasn't to know that the cobra had a large thorn stuck in its throat, or that her finger would dislodge the thorn and allow the snake to breathe freely again.

And so she was filled with amazement when, instead of biting her, the cobra said:

"You have saved my life, and in return for your great bravery and great kindness I shall do you as good a service."

The Ranee hung her head and confessed that the best service that he could do for her would be to bite her. However, little by little, the cobra coaxed the whole story from her, and then he smiled.

"You certainly did wrong to tell your husband such untruths," he said. "Nevertheless, you have helped me in my difficulty and I shall help you in yours. Bid your husband come here, and I shall provide you with parents of whom you shall have no cause to feel ashamed."

Hardly knowing what to think, the Ranee ordered the bearers to take her back to the palace, where she invited the Rajah to accompany her on a visit to the family home.

She could not believe her eyes when they reached the anthill. There, ahead of them, where previously there had been only thick jungle, stood a magnificent palace in extensive grounds. For as far as the eye could see there were gardens and orchards and fountains and ornamental bridges. The walls of the palace sparkled with precious stones and from every balcony there hung carpets of cloth of gold.

Hundreds of attendants in rich uniforms escorted them up the sweeping staircase and into the lofty throne room where an old Rajah and Ranee, seated on magnificent golden thrones, introduced themselves to the young man as his father-in-law and mother-in-law.

The young couple were entertained lavishly in the palace for six whole months before the young Rajah decided, reluctantly, that they should return home.

The old Rajah and Ranee showered them with costly gifts and ordered all the arrangements for the journey.

Just before it was time to set off, the young Ranee slipped away to find her friend, the cobra.

"You have worked marvels in conjuring up all these beautiful things to help me out of my difficulties," she said, "but my fears remain. Please don't think me ungrateful, but my husband has been so impressed and has enjoyed himself so much that he is sure to want to invite the Rajah and Ranee to his palace, or to want to visit them again some time."

The friendly cobra answered, "You have nothing to fear. All that will be taken care of, as you shall see if you turn to look back when you reach the waterfall."

The Ranee sat silently in her palanquin as the party set off back to the young Rajah's palace, wondering how the cobra could save her.

But at the waterfall she understood. The attendants began to shout and point back along their track. Looking behind, she could see the magnificent palace engulfed in smoke and flames.

Her husband immediately despatched some riders to help rescue the old Rajah and Ranee and their court, but it was too late; the building was reduced to rubble and ashes, and not a living creature remained.

The party returned home in sadness, but it was only natural that the Rajah's younger brother should ask about their wonderful, costly gifts, and talk to his wife about them.

His wife was intensely jealous when she heard the story and, of course, knew that there must have been some magic at work to explain these mysterious parents with their untold wealth.

"Why should my sister have such precious gifts all to herself?" she muttered. "I want my share, too."

When they were next alone she pestered her sister to tell her the truth about the visit, but the Ranee was reluctant to do so.

"You must tell me, I have a right to know," her sister stormed.

The Ranee wondered how she could talk like that when she had been responsible for their poor mother's death, but she didn't speak the thought aloud.

But after days and weeks of constant pestering from her sister, the Ranee gave in and told her about the cobra.

Her sister was triumphant. "I shall go to him," she declared, "and demand riches far more precious than anything you possess; just wait and see."

She lost no time in ordering a palanquin and setting off into the jungle.

There, by the white ants' nest, just as she had hoped, was the cobra, rearing up with mouth open.

She dismissed her bearers irritably and strode over to where the cobra sat. Without a fear in the world she thrust her finger into its mouth.

But he bit her and she died.

The Cat and the Mice

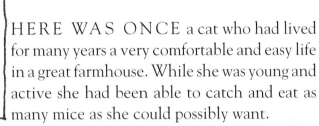

THERE WAS ONCE a cat who had lived for many years a very comfortable and easy life in a great farmhouse. While she was young and active she had been able to catch and eat as many mice as she could possibly want.

But now she was growing fat and getting short of breath, and she was finding it very difficult to catch any mice at all. One day she hit upon a sly plan. Calling up into the rafters, she begged all the mice to come down to the barn. And she promised that no harm would come to them.

When they were all gathered in front of her, she put on a humble expression and made a little speech.

"My dear friends," she said. "I am old and coming to the end of my life, so now is the time for me to set my conscience in order. Oh, yes; I freely admit it: I have been a very wicked cat."

The mice nodded in agreement, and wondered where this was leading.

"I know that I have brought fear to you all, young and old, and I am deeply ashamed of myself. But from now on I swear that I shall give up hunting mice."

The mice looked relieved to hear this.

"In return, I ask but one small favor, just to show that you forgive me and trust me. All I ask is that twice every day, once in the morning and once at night, you should file past me one by one, and make a little bow to show that there are no hard feelings. Now that isn't too much to ask, is it?"

The mice readily agreed that that was a small price to pay for their safety and peace of mind.

So that evening the cat took up her position on a sack of rice at one end of the barn and the mice trooped past her, one by one, entering from a crack in one barn wall and leaving by a crack in the other.

But it is a great mistake for a mouse to trust a cat. The cunning old creature had decided that she would nod and smile at every mouse as it passed, except for the last—which she would trap with her paw and gobble up.

"There are so many of them," she thought, "that no one will notice if a couple disappear every day."

And so she put her plan into action and, sure enough, for a few days she ate well without the bother of hunting.

Now, among the mice were two friends called Rambei and Ambei who were much brighter than all the others, and they soon suspected that something was not right.

So they put their heads together and decided that it would be a good thing if Rambei always headed the procession and Ambei always brought up the rear, and then they could keep calling to each other to make sure that everything was in order.

That night, just as Rambei had made his deep bow to the cat on her rice sack, he called out in his twittery voice:

"Are you there, brother Ambei?"

"I am indeed," came the equally twittery reply. "Right at the end of the line."

To the cat's intense irritation, the two of them kept up this conversation while all the mice trooped by, and prevented her from getting her supper.

The next morning, because she was feeling even hungrier, the cat was furious when the same thing happened again. But she forced herself to be patient.

"After all," she thought, "if they're such good friends they'll probably march together in the middle of the procession this evening. And perhaps there'll be an especially plump mouse at the end."

Imagine her rage when the performance was repeated, with Rambei and Ambei calling out to each other all the time.

That night Ambei, noticing how her claws were twitching with anger and frustration, told his friend what he'd seen.

The two of them decided that the time had come to warn the others to be ready for the cat to pounce.

Hunger pangs were now gnawing at the cat's stomach and her nerves were on edge. With Rambei's and Ambei's shrill little voices twittering in her ears, the cat's self-control snapped and she made a clumsy stab at the nearest mouse. But he was on his guard and was off like a flash through the crack in the wall.

Guessing now that the cat was in no condition to give chase, the mice spent the next few days up among the rafters.

The cat knew she was defeated and waddled off to find some other farm. And after that the mice lived very easily and, in gratitude to Rambei and Ambei, always let them have the place of honor on the rice sack.

Animal Language

THERE WAS ONCE a shepherd who had worked very faithfully for his master for many years.

One day, he was driving his master's flock of sheep through a wood on their way to the meadows when he heard a strange hissing noise.

He carefully crept up to the spot where the sounds seemed to be coming from and saw, to his surprise, a snake surrounded by a ring of fire.

The creature was obviously terrified by the leaping flames and, despite his mistrust of snakes, the man couldn't help feeling sorry for it.

After only a moment's hesitation the shepherd pushed his crook toward the snake, which immediately curled itself around it and began to slither along it, out of the heat of the flames.

But, to the shepherd's horror, it didn't drop off and dart away to safety; instead, it continued up the shepherd's arm and coiled itself around his neck.

The man broke into a cold sweat. "Is this the way you repay a good deed!" he cried. "I've saved your life, and now you're going to kill me in return."

"Nothing could be further from my thoughts," said the snake. "I'm truly grateful to you for rescuing me, but you must take me back to my father's house to receive your reward. My father, I must tell you, is the King of all snakes."

It was useless for the shepherd to plead that he didn't want a reward, all he wanted was for the snake to release him; the snake refused to loose his hold.

"But what about my sheep?" stammered the shepherd. "I can't leave them unattended. There are wolves about."

"I promise you that your sheep will come to no harm," said the snake. "And now, if you don't mind, we must go."

The trembling shepherd had no choice.

The snake directed his footsteps until at last they reached a door made of a solid mass of entwined snakes. At one quiet hiss from the Prince Snake they drew themselves back, leaving an opening for the shepherd to pass through.

"One word of advice before I present you to my father," the snake whispered in his ear. "In gratitude for your kindness toward me he is sure to offer you anything you care to name: gold, silver, precious stones. But you must insist that he grant you the power to understand animal language. He will try to change your mind; he will offer you all kinds of tempting gifts instead. And still you must insist that he give you the ability to understand animal language."

No sooner had he finished than two attendant-snakes came to escort them into the presence of the King Snake, who was overjoyed to hear how his son had been so narrowly rescued from death through the help of a stranger.

"Name your reward," he commanded. "No price is too high to pay for the life of my son."

"Your Majesty is very gracious," the shepherd muttered. "I would like to be able to understand the language of animals, if you don't mind."

"A mean gift to reward such a glorious act!" the King Snake exclaimed. "Why, I can offer you untold riches, fabulous palaces . . ."

Catching the eye of the Prince Snake, the shepherd summoned up his courage and insisted, "If you really intend to give me a reward then the gift of animal language is all I ask. If you cannot or will not grant me that, then I shall not bother you further but simply bid you farewell." And he turned to go.

"Stay!" ordered the King. "The gift of animal language is in my power, and since you will accept no other I must grant it to you. But be warned. It is a deadly gift, for if you reveal your secret to any other person you will instantly die."

The shepherd nodded to show that he understood and then, at the King Snake's command, opened his mouth. The King spat into it.

"Now spit into mine," he ordered. The shepherd did so, and the ceremony was repeated twice after that.

Then he was conducted through the door of entwined snakes and put on the path back to the woods. The last words that he heard from the King Snake were:

"The gift is a precious gift, and may good come of it. But guard your secret as you value your life."

The shepherd walked off in a daze, barely able to take in all the little snatches of conversation from the birds in the branches above his head and the little creatures in the tall grass at his feet.

Just as promised, he found his flock of sheep safe and sound in the very spot where he had left them. He was so overcome by the day's adventures that he sat down in the shade of a tree to think things over.

Before he quite knew what he was doing he found himself listening to the two ravens who had perched overhead.

"Life is strange," said one raven to the other. "This shepherd is a poor, hard-working man, and yet his sheep are grazing on untold wealth."

"True," said the other. "If only he knew what was buried beneath the spot where the black lamb is standing!"

The shepherd was a very faithful servant and immediately reported what he had heard to his master when he returned that evening. But, of course, he was careful not to say how he had heard it.

The master provided a cart and the two of them drove to the wood the next morning and started to dig. In no time they had unearthed several large metal chests, all crammed with shining gold and silver coins.

They couldn't believe their eyes. The master, who was as honest as the shepherd was loyal, was the first to speak.

"This treasure belongs to you and you alone," he said. "Use it wisely, and use it well. My advice to you is to build a house, take a wife, and start a business to keep you occupied and happy."

And the shepherd did just as his master had advised him. They were sad to part company, but at least they parted good friends.

By spending his money sensibly the shepherd became, in time, the wealthiest man in the whole district, employing farm-workers, cattle-drivers, and shepherds of his own.

A few days before Christmas he said to his wife, "Let's prepare a feast and travel out tomorrow to our farthest farm, to give our servants a good treat."

His wife rallied the kitchen staff and filled several hampers with delicious things to eat and drink.

The master sat down with the servants for the first part of the festivities, but then he rose and said, partly out of generosity and partly for old times' sake, "I will be on the watch with the dogs tonight. Enjoy your feast."

He wrapped himself up warmly and set off with the farm dogs to keep a lookout for prowling wolves. Just before midnight he heard a solitary wolf howling, but it wasn't just howling to him, of course; he could understand what the wolf was saying.

"Listen, dogs," it said. "Why not let us slip into the sheepfold and slaughter a few sheep. We promise to leave some dead animals for you. After all, your masters are feasting tonight, so why shouldn't you?"

Most of the dogs were delighted by the idea and barked back in agreement, but one almost toothless old dog who had belonged to the master when he was just a simple shepherd barked back in defiance.

"Just try," he shouted. "While I've still got two teeth in my head no mangy wolf is going to lay a claw on my master's sheep."

The other dogs exchanged guilty looks and the wolf fell silent.

The next morning, before he set out for home, the master gave orders that all the dogs on the estate, except the old one, should be killed. The servants were amazed as this was so unlike him, but they could see that he was serious and did as he had ordered.

The master rode his horse hard, in a gloomy mood. Behind him his wife, riding a mare, had to keep urging it to keep up with her husband.

When they were just about at the halfway point the master's horse drew to a halt, looked over its shoulder and whinnied to the mare:

"Get a move on. Why are you lagging behind?"

"It's all very well for you with the master in the saddle. Our mistress, I grant you, is a very good pastry cook, but she not only bakes more cakes than anyone else in the district, she *eats* more too!"

As the mare drew up alongside her companion the wife noticed that her husband was grinning broadly. Pleased to see him happy again after the miserable start to the day she asked him what he was smiling at.

"Oh, it's nothing," he said, coaxing the horse forward again.

"It must be something," she said. "Go on, tell me."

"I really can't tell you, dear," he replied.

"What do you mean 'can't'?" she stormed.

The wretched man found himself in a very difficult situation.

"Well, I *could* tell you," he said, "but please believe me, if I told you I'd drop down dead."

"I demand to know," his wife shouted. "If you refuse to share a little joke with your wife then I'll know for certain that you don't really love me."

The husband felt very upset at this and decided that he must show his wife how much he really loved her, despite the terrible price he would have to pay. At least he persuaded her to be patient until they reached home.

As soon as they arrived the man ordered his carpenter to knock up a coffin and place it in the courtyard.

Then the man said to his wife, "I shall lie in the coffin to tell you what it was that made me smile. And after I've told you I shall die."

Just as he was about to lie down he saw his faithful old dog padding toward him, with a tear in its eye, and asked his wife to give it a dish of bread soaked in milk. The dog halfheartedly wagged its moth-eaten tail in gratitude but couldn't bring itself to taste even a mouthful. Seeing this, the farmyard rooster came strutting up and started tucking in.

"Pity to see it wasted," he said to the dog between pecks.

"How can you!" wailed the dog. "Have you no pity at all for the master. Can't you see that he's just about to die simply to satisfy his wife's curiosity?"

"If he's as big a fool as that," retorted the rooster, "the world won't miss him. I've got over a hundred wives and if I find a tasty grain of corn in the yard I cluck-cluck-cluck until they all come running, and then I eat it myself. Just to show who's boss. And that booby can't even manage a single wife."

Hearing this, the man suddenly changed his mind and leapt out of the coffin.

"Just come a bit closer, my dear," he thundered, "and I'll tell you my little joke."

Alarmed to see her husband in this unusual threatening mood the wife ran away and hid in the cowshed until dusk, when he seemed to have calmed down and she thought it safe to come out.

She never asked him an awkward question after that, and they lived happily ever after.

The Rabbit and the Elephants

MANY, MANY YEARS AGO there was a terrible drought and all the elephants were desperate for a drink of water. The King Elephant sent out the healthier young elephants to the furthest corners of the country to search far and wide for a stream or a pond.

One by one they returned, dragging themselves across the parched earth, only to report that they had had no success. Until, finally, the last of the elephants arrived through the dust and announced that many weary miles away he had found a beautiful pool fed by a spring, known as the Fountain of the Moon.

There was no time to lose. The King Elephant summoned his subjects and they set off on their long, slow journey to the Fountain of the Moon, traveling by night and resting in the shade by day.

When they at last arrived they could hardly believe their eyes. The water was fresh tasting, the grass around the pool was green and tender, and the trees provided welcome shade.

When the elephants had drunk as much as they wanted the King Elephant proclaimed that this was the most perfect spot on earth and that they would never leave it.

Now the elephants weren't the only creatures to think that the pool was an ideal place to live. For as long as anyone could remember the rabbits had had their burrows beneath the meadows around it, and they were very alarmed by the sudden arrival of the newcomers.

The King Rabbit called a meeting in his underground hall.

"Unless we can find a way to make the elephants move on," he declared, "it will be a disaster for us rabbits. They have been here only three days but already they have eaten most of our grass and, what's even more serious, they are beginning to make our tunnels collapse with their trampling to and fro."

The rabbits nodded solemnly. The situation was very serious indeed.

"I will bestow the highest honors upon anyone who succeeds in removing this terrible threat to our safety," the King Rabbit continued.

There was complete silence. Every rabbit wanted the elephants to go, and every rabbit wanted to be honored by the King; but nobody had the least idea of what could be done about it.

Nobody, that is, except one. A little rabbit, seeing that the others weren't going to make any suggestions, timidly raised his paw.

"You have our permission to speak," said the King Rabbit gravely, and all heads turned toward the little rabbit.

"If Your Majesty would allow me to leave the burrow tonight, I believe I could persuade the elephants to move on."

The other rabbits exchanged glances and sniggered.

"Who else has a suggestion?" asked the King Rabbit severely. That shut them up.

Turning to the little rabbit the King Rabbit went on:

"My son, you have our permission and our thanks. Be bold but don't be rash. And remember, you represent your King in this undertaking."

The little rabbit bowed, "I shall do my best not to let you down, Your Majesty," he said.

That night the little rabbit squeezed out of a hole under a bush and crept over to where the elephants were still eating.

He had no intention of getting too close. If one of them should step on him in the dark he would be squashed flat.

Instead, he scrambled up the nearest tree and hid himself in the leaves. Looking down, he had a clear view of the King Elephant.

In his loudest and deepest voice (which wasn't so very deep) he suddenly called out:

"Oh, hear me, dishonorable King of the Elephants."

The King Elephant looked around him angrily, and the other elephants stopped chewing.

"Know that I am the Ambassador of the Moon," the little rabbit went on, "the Moon whom you claim to respect. But you do not deceive our great mistress. She knows how little you care for the smaller creatures under her protection, and she is angry with you."

The King Elephant was standing quite still now, looking rather anxious.

"The Moon knows that you have become too full of your own importance, and she is deciding whether to punish you or not."

At this the other elephants began looking at their King reproachfully.

"If you will not take my word for it, you have only to gaze on the Moon's royal face in her own fountain."

The King Elephant tiptoed over to the pool and looked down at the reflection of the Moon on the still surface of the water.

"Take some water to wash yourself with, pay your respects, and perhaps–who knows?–the Moon will pardon you."

The King Elephant lowered his trunk into the pool, disturbing the smooth surface as he did so. He was just about to spray the water over his back when the little rabbit called out:

"I see it is too late. The Moon is so offended by your inconsiderate behavior that she has shivered into a thousand pieces and is trembling with rage."

The King Elephant took one quick look into the pool.

"What the Ambassador of the Moon says is true," he trumpeted to the others. "Let us hang our heads in shame and leave as quickly as we can, in the hope of escaping some terrible punishment."

And with a thundering of feet that brought the earth cascading down in the burrows below, the elephants lumbered off into the night.

Out of gratitude the King Rabbit gave the little rabbit the title of Rabbit Extraordinary, and after that mother rabbits would always point him out to their children as the rabbit who frightened off the elephants.

A World of Folktales

A remarkable thing about folktales, as you may already have discovered for yourself, is how often you can find the same story, with only small variations, in very different parts of the world.

There are many reasons for this: the stories might resemble each other out of pure coincidence; or the storytellers might have traveled or migrated, taking their stories with them; or, in more recent times, the stories might have spread through books.

For the animal tales in this collection I have generally kept quite close to versions that were being told and written down at the end of the nineteenth century and at the start of the twentieth century, although the tales themselves are, for the most part, very much older than that, of course.

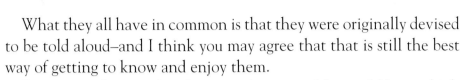

What they all have in common is that they were originally devised to be told aloud–and I think you may agree that that is still the best way of getting to know and enjoy them.

For interest, here is a brief note on the parts of the world from which the stories in this book were collected.

How the Turtle Got His Shell comes from what is now Papua New Guinea.

The Coyote and the Ravens and *The Turkey Girl* were both told by the Zuñi, Pueblo Indians from around the Zuñi River in New Mexico.

The Singing Tortoise was collected from Ghana (in West Africa) when it was known as the Gold Coast.

The Ranee and the Cobra and *The Crocodile and the Jackal* are Hindi stories heard in the Deccan, in central India.

The Impudent Little Bird flew in from Spain.

Animal Language, in this version, is from a Serbian source (before Serbia ever became part of what we knew until recently as Yugoslavia) but it is found in nearly every Slavonic language.

The Cat and the Mice come from Tibet.

The Young Leopard and the Ram belong to the folklore of the nomadic Hottentots of southwestern Africa.

The Rabbit and the Elephants has the oldest recorded history of all the tales in this book, appearing in a collection of fables known as the *Panchatantra* by Bidpay (or Pilpay, as he is sometimes called) which was translated as long ago as the sixth century AD into Persian, and then into Arabic. Nothing, however, is recorded about Bidpay–and many people believe he might himself be a bit of a fable!